Lucy and the Gift-Wrapped Guests

John Stadler

WARNER
JUVENILE
BOOKS

A Warner Communications Company

New York

Warner Books, Inc., 666 Fifth Avenue, New York, NY 10103

 A Warner Communications Company

Printed in the United States of America
First Warner Juvenile Books Printing: November 1989
10 9 8 7 6 5 4 3 2 1

Library of Congress Cataloging-in-Publication Data
Stadler, John.
    Lucy and the gift-wrapped guests / by John Stadler — Warner
juvenile books ed.
        p.   cm.
    Summary: Lucy's friends Liz and Izzy, two juggling mice, help her
deal with the influx of alligators which is ruining business at her
hotel.
    ISBN 1-55782-048-1
    [1. Hotels, motels, etc. — Fiction.   2. Alligators — Fiction.
3. Mice — Fiction.   4. Stories in rhyme.]   I. Title.
PZ8.3.S7814Lu   1989
[E] — dc20   88-40820
                                            CIP
                                            AC

For Joe

Whiskers and his family were staying at the Hotel Lucy. One night as he was tucking in his grandchildren, one of them said, "Sing us a song before we go to sleep, Grandpa!"

Whiskers pulled out his ukelele, saying, "Here's one about how this hotel got its start. It goes like this:"

Lucy was a little girl
Who loved hotels the most.
She bought herself a nice one
Along a sunny coast.

Lucy had all kinds of guests
Who came from everywhere.
They came to swim or play or sun,
Or just to take the air.

Lucy's guests were healthy;
She served them fresh brown rice.
She had two twins in her employ
And they were both gray mice.

Before they came to Lucy's place
Their lives had been a struggle.
But now they were so popular
Because they loved to juggle.

Yes, Liz and Izzy juggled.
They juggled day and night.
They juggled with all kinds of things,
With anything in sight.

Now the mayor of the village,
Who owned most every store,
Had everything that he could want—
But still he wanted more.

He came to visit Lucy
And said, "I want your land.
Give it to me right away
Or I'll blast it all to sand!"

Lucy laughed and said, "No way!
This place is mine for keeps.
Get off my land, you awful man.
You'll give my guests the creeps."

"You had your chance," the mayor said,
"And I won't let you stay.
I'll get both your hotel and land.
I *always* get my way!"

Soon enough the doorbell rang;
Lucy jumped down from her chair.
She opened up the front door wide
To find a gator there.

"My name is Clyde. How do you do?"
The alligator said.
Lucy answered, "Fine, I guess."
Her heart was filled with dread.

"I want to stay in your hotel,"
Said the alligator.
"Some friends of mine are coming, too.
I think they'll be here later."

"You're welcome here," Lucy said,
Feeling rather nervous.
"I hope that you enjoy your stay
And I am at your service."

Clyde sat right down at the table
And ate just like a shark,
Talking on quite endlessly
Till day gave way to dark.

Early dawn the doorbell rang.
Lucy opened up the door.
Standing there in front of her
Were gators: twenty-four!

The gators made an awful scene.
They ran about the halls.
They screamed and jumped and danced and sang
And hit their tennis balls.

Things just went from bad to worse
On that dreadful day.
All the guests got in their cars
And quickly drove away.

The front bell rang and Lucy ran
To open up the door.
Standing there with toothy grins
Were gators: plenty more!

Lucy took their bags and said,
"I guess I'll have to try it.
But it looks to me as if I've got
A full-scale gator riot."

There were gators on the chandeliers
And gators wearing skis.
There were gators in the hot tubs
And gators in the trees.

CAUTION! Hot Tub In Use!

Lucy said, "This is bad.
It's time to take a stand.
Liz and you, too, Izzy,
Won't you lend a hand?"

The mice, they came on over,
Standing twin to twin.
"All right!" said Lucy boldly,
"Begin, you mice, to spin!"

They picked up every gator,
Juggling them with ease,
Until the gators cried as one,
"Put us down! Oh, please!!!"

Lucy said, "You can't come down.
You'll stay up high, I fear.
Unless you tell us why you've come
And what you're doing here."

The gators spun round and round,
Thanks to Liz and Izzy.
Clyde called out, "I'll tell the truth,
Though I'm rather dizzy."

"We really do apologize,"
Said Clyde atop the pile,
"Being mean and thoughtless
Is really not our style.

"The mayor said," the gator sighed,
"To come and bother you.
Or otherwise, he'd take us all
And throw us in a zoo.

"He said if we were bad enough
Then you would want to sell.
At last," said Clyde the gator,
"He could have your fine hotel."

"I need your help," said Lucy,
"For I have something planned."
"Absolutely," Clyde replied,
"Your wish is our command."

The next day, Lucy, Liz and Izzy
Were creeping 'round like foxes,
Carrying high upon their backs
Fifty gift-wrapped boxes.

They knocked upon the mayor's door
And then they yelled, "SURPRISE!"
"I guess that it's my birthday,"
He said and rubbed his eyes.

He took the boxes on inside
And yelled, "Now go away!"
So Lucy, Liz and Izzy
Left him there that day.

The mayor opened up his gifts
With greed and great delight.
But the gators waiting there inside
Gave the man a fright.

From that day on, the gators
Were loved around the town.
And Lucy was delighted
Each time they came around.

And the mayor of the village,
The gators put in jail.
Now someone new is mayor.
He's green and has a tail.

Whiskers put down his ukelele. Just then there was a knock at the door and in walked a guest. "Could you knock off the music, pal?! It's late and some of us are trying to get some sleep!"